A Trip to Grandma's

by C.L. Reid

illustrated by Elena Aiello

PICTURE WINDOW BOOKS
a capstone imprint

Published by Picture Window Books, an imprint of Capstone
1710 Roe Crest Drive, North Mankato, Minnesota 56003
capstonepub.com

Library of Congress Cataloging-in-Publication Data
Names: Reid, C. L., author. | Aiello, Elena (Illustrator), illustrator. |
Reid, C. L. Emma every day.
Title: A trip to Grandma's / by C. L. Reid ; illustrated by Elena Aiello.
Description: North Mankato, Minnesota : Picture Window Books, an
imprint of Capstone, 2022. | Series: Emma every day |
Audience: Ages 5-7. | Audience: Grades K-1. |
Summary: Emma and her brother are staying at their
grandmother's house for a full week; she has packed her favorite
stuffed toy and the recharger for her cochlear implant, but she is
a little worried about feeling homesick—but with her grandmother
keeping her busy, and the help of a new deaf friend named
Nick, the week flies by. Includes an ASL fingerspelling chart,
glossary, and content-related questions.
Identifiers: LCCN 2021006175 (print) | LCCN 2021006176 (ebook)
| ISBN 9781663909305 (hardcover) | ISBN 9781663921949
(paperback) | ISBN 9781663909275 (pdf) Subjects: LCSH: Deaf
children—Juvenile fiction. | Cochlear implants—Juvenile fiction. |
Grandmothers—Juvenile fiction. | Grandparent and child—Juvenile
fiction. | Friendship—Juvenile fiction. | CYAC: Deaf—Fiction. | People
with disabilities—Fiction. | Grandmothers—Fiction. | Friendship—
Fiction. | Cochlear implants—Fiction. Classification: LCC PZ7.1.R4544
Tr 2021 (print) | LCC PZ7.1.R4544 (ebook) | DDC [E]—dc23
LC record available at https://lccn.loc.gov/2021006175
LC ebook record available at https://lccn.loc.gov/2021006176

Image Credits: Capstone: Daniel Griffo, bottom right 28, bottom
right 29, Margeaux Lucas, top right 28, Randy Chewning, top left 28,
bottom left 28, top left 29, top right 29, bottom left 29

Design Elements: Shutterstock: achii, Mari C, Mika Besfamilnaya

Special thanks to Evelyn Keolian for her consulting work.

Designer: Tracy Davies

Printed and bound in the United States of America. PO4270

TABLE OF CONTENTS

MEET EMMA

EMMA CARTER
Age: 8 Grade: 3

SIBLING
one brother, Jaden
(12 years old)

PARENTS
David and Lucy

BEST FRIEND
Izzie Jackson

PET
a goldfish named Ruby

favorite color: **teal**
favorite food: **tacos**
favorite school subject: **writing**
favorite sport: **swimming**
hobbies: **reading, writing, biking, swimming**

FINGERSPELLING GUIDE

MANUAL ALPHABET

Aa   Bb   Cc   Dd   Ee

Ff   Gg   Hh   Ii   Jj

MANUAL NUMBERS

0   1   2   3

Emma is Deaf. She uses American Sign Language (ASL) to communicate with her family. She also uses a cochlear implant (CI) to help her hear some sounds.

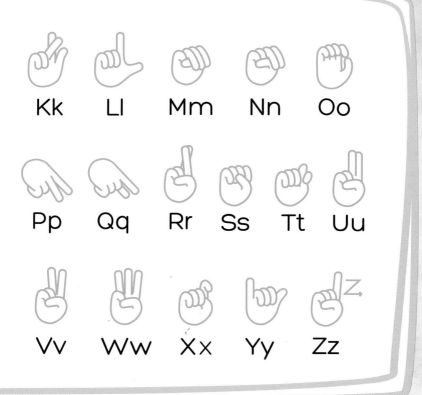

Kk   Ll   Mm   Nn   Oo

Pp   Qq   Rr   Ss   Tt   Uu

Vv   Ww   Xx   Yy   Zz

④   ⑤   ⑥   ⑦   ⑧   ⑨   ⑩

Chapter 1
The Big Welcome

"Do I have everything?" Emma

asked Ruby, her pet fish.

She looked around and picked

up her favorite stuffed animal.

"Oops!  I can't forget Fluffy or this stuff," she said.

She put the batteries and charger for her cochlear implant (CI) into her bag.

"I think that's it," Emma said. "Bye, Ruby."

Emma was going to stay with her grandma for a week. She was very excited, but she was nervous too.

After a few hours, the car stopped in front of Grandma's house. Emma and Jaden hopped out.

"Have a good week," Dad signed.

He hugged Emma and Jaden.

"Have fun  with

Grandma," Mom signed. She gave

them both a big hug too.

"I love you," Emma signed.

She blinked back tears and tried
to smile as she waved goodbye.

"Let's go in the house and eat.
I made spaghetti, meatballs, and
cookies," Grandma signed.

Emma wasn't sure she could eat.
Her stomach hurt.

Chapter 2
Homesick

That night, Emma had a hard time falling asleep. When she did sleep, she dreamed that something terrible had happened to Ruby.

Emma grabbed Fluffy and ran to Grandma's room.

"I think something bad happened to Ruby," Emma signed.

"Ruby is okay. You had a nightmare," Grandma signed. "You can sleep with me."

When Emma woke up the next morning, she put on her CI and went into the kitchen. Emma wasn't hungry for breakfast.

Just then, Muffin, Grandma's sweet cat, rubbed against her leg.

"I miss Ruby," she said.

"It's a nice day. Let's go weed my flower garden," Grandma said.

"Mom would love these flowers," Emma signed.

"You can take some home for her," Grandma signed.

It was raining the next day.

Grandma said, "Let's drive into town today. I need to buy cat food, and you can each pick out a toy."

They each got a yo-yo.

The third day Grandma said,

"Let's work in my vegetable garden

today. You can pick ripe vegetables."

"Dad would like these vegetables,"

Emma signed.

"You can take some home for

him," Grandma signed.

Chapter 3
A New Friend

The next day, Emma and Jaden

stood on Grandma's front porch.

Emma played with her new yo-yo.

She liked being with Grandma,

but she was ready to go home. Just

then a kid carrying a soccer ball

walked up the driveway, waving at

Emma and Jaden.

"Hello, my name is Nick," the boy signed. "What are your names?"

"Emma and my brother, Jaden," Emma signed. "Are you deaf?"

"Yes. Are you deaf?" Nick signed.

"Yes. I use a CI," Emma signed.

"Jaden is hearing. We are visiting my grandma."

Grandma stepped out onto the porch, smiling.

"Hello, Nick. How are you?" she signed.

"Great!" he signed.

Grandma looked at Emma and Jaden. "Nick moved here a few months ago," she signed.

"Cool," Emma fingerspelled.

"You want to play soccer?" Nick signed, looking excited.

"Yes!" Jaden and Emma signed at the same time.

Emma, Jaden, and Nick played soccer for an hour. Emma forgot all about feeling homesick.

That night after dinner Jaden signed, "Let's watch a movie."

"I will make popcorn and lemonade," Grandma said.

Emma sat on the couch beside Grandma. She munched on popcorn as they watched the movie with the closed captions (CC) on the TV.

"I can't wait until I can come back and visit you," Emma signed.

"Anytime, sweetie. Anytime," Grandma signed.

LEARN TO SIGN

sleep

Close hand in front of face.

night

Move hand down
and away from body.

grandmother

1. Make the sign for "mother."
2. Bounce hand away from chin.

sad

Move hands down in
front of face.

blanket

Bring hands to shoulders.

cook

Move hand back and forth.

cookie

Rotate C shape.

I love you

Combine the shapes I, L, and Y.

GLOSSARY

closed captions (CC)—the text version of what is being said or heard (such as a doorbell, knocking, music, etc.) on the TV show or movie that is shown on the screen

cochlear implant (also called CI)—a device that helps someone who is Deaf to hear; it is worn on the head just above the ear

deaf—being unable to hear

fingerspell—to make letters with your hands to spell out words; often used for names of people and places

homesick—missing your home

nervous—feeling worried

sign language—a language in which hand gestures, along with facial expressions and body movements, are used to communicate

TALK ABOUT IT

1. Would you like to be away from your home for a week? Why or why not?

2. How do you think Emma felt when her parents left?

3. Talk about some things you can do when you feel nervous.

WRITE ABOUT IT

1. Make a list of three places you would like to go for a week. Then make a list of all the items you would bring to each place.

2. Emma feels nervous being away from home. Write about a time you felt nervous.

3. Pretend you are Emma. Write a thank-you note to Grandma for your fun week.

Ruby

ABOUT THE AUTHOR

Deaf-blind since childhood, C.L. Reid received a cochlear implant (CI) as an adult to help her hear, and she uses American Sign Language (ASL) to communicate. She and her husband have three sons. Their middle son is also deaf-blind. C.L. earned a master's degree in writing for children and young adults at Hamline University in St. Paul, Minnesota. She lives in Minnesota with her husband, two of their sons, and their cats.

ABOUT THE ILLUSTRATOR

Elena Aiello is an illustrator and character designer. After graduating as a marketing specialist, she decided to study art direction and CGI. Doing so, she discovered a passion for illustration and conceptual art. She works as a freelancer for various magazines and publishers. Elena loves video games and sushi. She lives with her husband and her little pug, Gordon, in Milan, Italy.